With thanks to my family: Benedict, George, and Nigel.
Also to Jane Green, Sarah Davies from the Holy Trinity Pewley
Down School in Guildford, and the National Autistic Society.
And for all the encouragement and support from Denise Johnstone-Burt
and all at Walker Books, and my agent, Laura Cecil.

First U.S. edition 2016

Library of Congress Catalog Card Number 2015934768
ISBN 978-0-7636-8121-0

15 16 17 18 19 20 APS 10 9 8 7 6 5 4 3 2 1

Printed in Humen, Dongguan, China

This book was typeset in WB Walsh.
The illustrations were done in acrylic.

Candlewick Press
99 Dover Street
Somerville, Massachusetts 02144

visit us at www.candlewick.com

Isaac and His Amazing Asperger Superpowers!

melanie walsh

CANDLEWICK PRESS

My name is Isaac, and I'm a superhero!

You might think I look just like everyone else, but I've got special superpowers that make me slightly different from my brother and the other kids at school. However, some children don't understand this and call me names.

My superhero brain is fantastic and remembers loads of things. I love to tell people interesting facts I know,

cat
rocket
snake

600

but sometimes they don't seem to be
interested in the same things as me!

My superpowers give me lots of energy, and I love to bounce around on my trampoline for hours! It makes me feel happy.

Sometimes at school my teacher asks if I want to play soccer. But I don't like running around, and superheroes don't like sticky mud.

Oh . . . hello.

Because I'm a superhero,
I have lots of things
to think about.
I try to remember
to be friendly
and say hello to
people I know, but
sometimes I forget.
I'm not being rude.

My pets understand me and my
superpowers, and I love them.
I find it easy to talk to them
because they always listen to me
and love me as I am.

Because my teacher knows I'm a superhero, she lets me fidget with my special toy in class. It helps me feel calm and I can listen better.

"Meow," said the little cat.
"Shh," said Mommy.

Shh!

As a superhero, I tend to say whatever comes into my head!

My mom says that I should try to keep these thoughts inside my head so that I don't upset people.

Superheroes listen carefully, but sometimes get confused. When my brother told me that my tummy would go POP if I ate too much . . .

I believed him!
I don't really get
jokes like that.

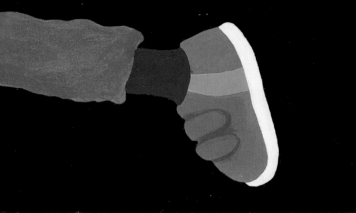

that some lights make in school. This makes my ears really hurt, and then I feel upset.

I feel scared
when I look people
in the eyes.

My dad taught me a good
superhero trick. I just look
at people's foreheads instead.
It really works!

Superheroes are really good at spotting things.
At recess, if there isn't a game I want to play,
I like to use my super vision to find interesting
things that other people haven't seen!

You may not have guessed, but I'm not really a superhero. I have Asperger's (it rhymes with hamburgers), which is a kind of autism.

You can't catch it. It just means my brain works a little differently.

But I do love
playing superheroes
with my brother.
He understands
me, and now
you do too!